DIVE INTO THE DEEP END

with more inflatable adventures!

THE INFLATABLES in MISSION UN-POPPABLE

By Beth Garrod & Jess Hitchman
Illustrated by Chris Danger

Scholastic Inc.

To the greatest ever writer, my mum −JH

For Daddles, the original and best storyteller −BG

To my fiancé, my adventure partner, and the love of my life, Eva. I love you more than Donut loves snacks. −CD

Text copyright © 2022 by Beth Garrod & Jess Hitchman

Illustrations copyright © 2022 by Chris Danger

All rights reserved. Published by Scholastic Inc., *Publishers since 1920.* SCHOLASTIC and associated logos are trademarks and/or registered trademarks of Scholastic Inc.

The publisher does not have any control over and does not assume any responsibility for author or third-party websites or their content.

This book is a work of fiction. Names, characters, places, and incidents are either the product of the author's imagination or are used fictitiously, and any resemblance to actual persons, living or dead, business establishments, events, or locales is entirely coincidental.

ISBN 978-1-338-74899-4

10 9 8 7 6 5 4 3 2 1   22 23 24 25 26

Printed in the U.S.A.   37

First printing, 2022

Book design by Stephanie Yang

And THAT'S how you make perfect nonstop-pop-a-lot popcorn.

POP

It's . . . POP . . . the best . . . POP . . . invention . . . POP . . . in the chewniverse!

POP POP POP

I SOUND LIKE **A MONSTER.**

VOICE DISGUISE 5000

And now I sound like a tiny fly.

OMG I'm so cute!

BUT I'M ALSO **VERY SCARY.**

Things are going swimmingly for me. To the infinity pool and beyond! Thanks, Cactus!

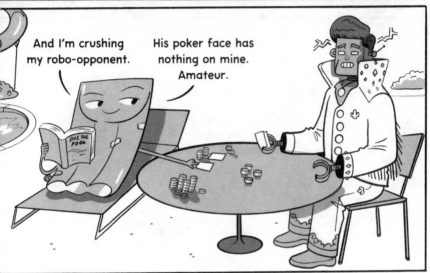

And I'm crushing my robo-opponent.

His poker face has nothing on mine. Amateur.

LYNN'S HAPPY FACE

LYNN'S SAD FACE

LYNN'S POKER FACE

5

Sweet! I normally have to buy surprise gifts for myself. Wait! I think I forgot my July-versary!

Your what?

DONUT'S MONTH-IVERSARY GIFTS (TO HIMSELF)

JANU-VERSARY

FEBRU-VERSARY

MARCH-VERSARY

APRIL-VERSARY

EXTRA-APRIL-VERSARY

MAY-VERSARY

13

15

17

Now you can bend into any shape you like!

FLAMINGO
MODELING KIT

No. 27 | SUPER CUTE PUPPY!

STEP 1: PUT YOUR HEAD BEHIND YOUR TAIL.

STEP 2: TUCK YOUR LEFT WING BEHIND YOUR NECK.

STEP 3: SAY "I LOVE AVOCADOS" THREE TIMES.

I LOVE AVOCADOS, I LOVE...

STEP 4: POINT YOUR BEAK TO THE LEFT.

STEP 5: TA-DA! YOU'RE A PUPPY.

SPECIAL BENDY MODELING SPRAY INCLUDED

23

Chapter Three
An Air-Raising Experiment

Cactus was in her element.

THE WORLD'S MOS
COMPLICATED SCIEN
EXPERIMENT

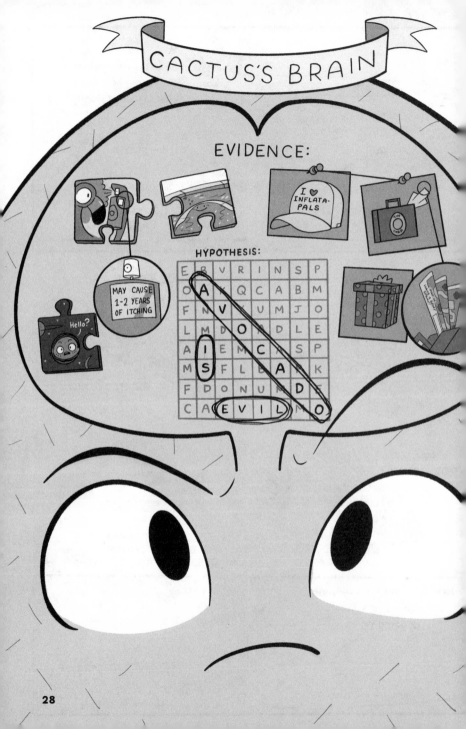

Time to un-sink Donut and his belly full of churros.

Bite infinity and eleven . . .
Bite infinity and twelve . . .

31

What for, Cactus?

Saving you from evil Avocado's dastardly deeds!

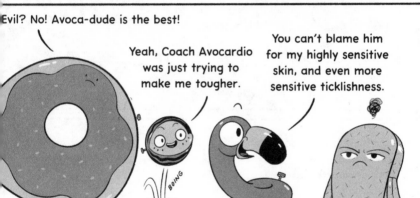

Evil? No! Avoca-dude is the best!

Yeah, Coach Avocardio was just trying to make me tougher.

You can't blame him for my highly sensitive skin, and even more sensitive ticklishness.

BOING

To be honest, Cactus, you're being kinda . . . prickly.

Prickly? Me?

33

Chapter Four

An Air of Mystery

Cactus was feeling deflated. But she had a point to prove.

Has anyone seen Avocado?

BE BACK SOON!
Love,
FROM YOUR FRIENDLY AVOCADO
XOXO

He said he had to do something normal and un-suspicious, and went thataway.

Weird coincidence! That's just where I was heading . . .

WOBBLE WOBBLE

WOBBLE GOGGLES
Can see around corners, above buildings, and down water slides

STAFF ONLY
WALTER S. LIDE'S
BATHING TRUNKS
COLLECTION

WOBBLE GOGGLE
EXTENDED MOD

What IS he avoca-doing?

Avocado might be a fruit full of nutrients, but he's up to something. Well, here goes nothing . . .

Hello-oooo-hhhhh? Is there an unexpected yet totally welcome stranger in here?

Mysterious. I thought I heard someone snooping around.

And if there's one thing Avocado doesn't like, it's snoopers. Or huggers. Or smoothie blenders.

And don't get me started on smelly balls of fur with air holes under their tails. What's the word for them? Oh, yes . . . cats.

Here, vile smelly-welly. I mean, cute kitty-catty. Eat this and stay away from me. I've got evil plans to be getting on with.

57 STEP EVIL PLAN TO TAKE OVER HAVE A GREAT SPRAY

STEP 7: BAN HUGS!

Who said that?!

Evil plans! I KNEW it!

Me!

You've met your match, Avocado! As long as I'm inflated, you're not going to get away with any evil plans. So hand over that book . . .

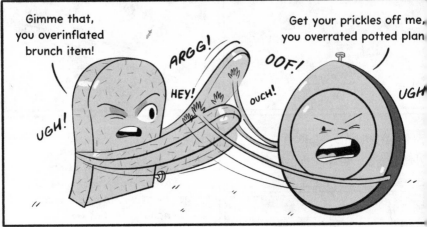

Gimme that, you overinflated brunch item!

UGH!

ARGG!

HEY!

OUCH!

OOF!

UGH!

Get your prickles off me, you overrated potted plan

I could eat you on toast!

DASTARDLY PLANS

SCHOLASTIC

DASTARDLY PLANS

Says the plant everyone forget to water.

40

Give up, Avocado! The game's over.

No, my silly little succulent! It's only just BEGUN!

It's time for you and the rest of your inflata-dweebs to meet the real me . . .

SWIPE
SWIPE
SWIPE

AVOCADON'T!!!!

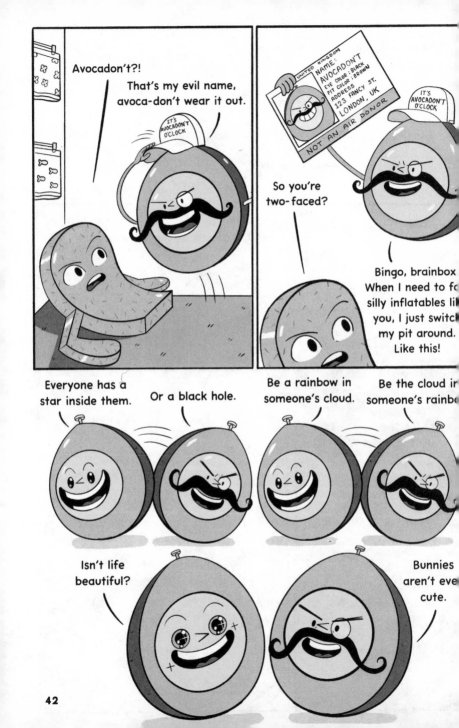

43

Chapter Five
Oh, No You Avoca-don't!

Inflata-pals!! Hold on to your air holes! You'll never believe what I just discovered!

Avocado ISN'T an innocent inflatable! He's an EVIL MASTERMIND! With a surprisingly long mustache!!!!

AND HE PLANS TO TAKE OVER THE PARK!

Um . . .
anyone?

Well, I for one
am furious.

You made me miss grabbing
the golden nacho! I've been
stalking that sucker for hours.

But there is no excuse for a
surprisingly long mustache.

45

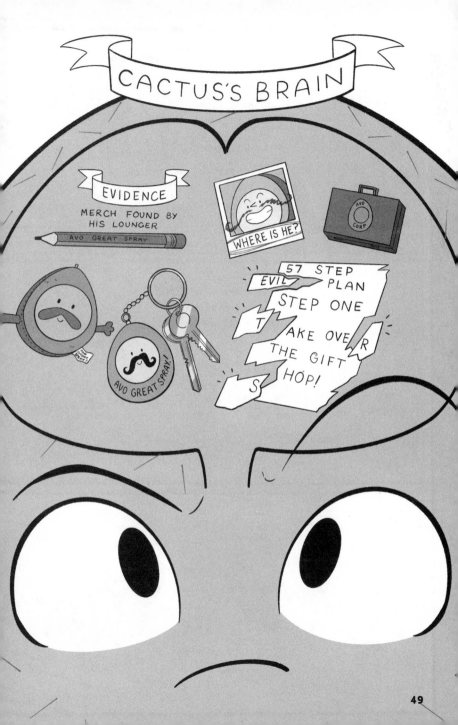

50

Oh, what sweet kitty-witties.

I mean vile-smelly-wellies.

SWISH SWISH

I need you outta my way so I can get to the gift shop.

CATS STINK!

FWWW

CATS STINK

CATS STINK

GNAWS! JAWS!

53

THE LAWS OF GNAWS AND JAWS

GNAWS (OR JAWS)

JAWS (OR GNAWS)

WAG WAG

RAZOR-SHARP LIKE CACTUS'S BRAIN

SMOOTH, LIKE MELTED ICE CREAM

MATCHING BUTTS! COOL!

55

PILLOW FIGHT

WATER FIGHT

STARING CONTEST

THUMB WAR

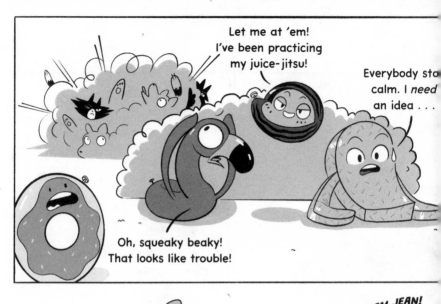

UPSICLES + MAGNIFYING GLASS + SUN =

IPPERIEST GOOP TO STOP AVOCADON'T

ICE CREAM
JEAN

ICE CR
S JE

LAP
LAP

SCHLURP!

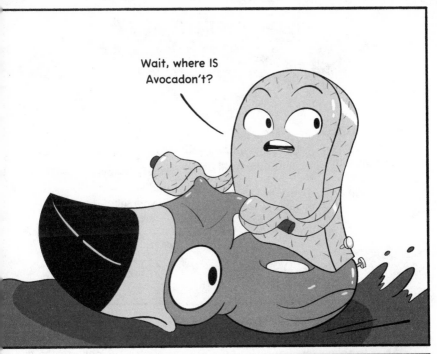

Chapter Seven

Eggs-It Through the Gift Shop

You put your air hole in! You put your air hole out!

You put your air hole in! And you shake it all about.

You do the Floaty Pokey, and you turn yourself around.

GUYS!! THIS NOT WHAT ALL ABOU

We don't have time for silly dances. Avocadon't has gone to the gift shop to take over the world!

Dude, he's probably gone to the gift shop to pee.

MIND. BLOWN.

Trembling test tubes! Avocadon't already made a whole new catalog for the gift shop!

Wait— inflatab pee?

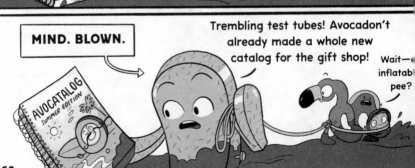

AVOCATALOG SUMMER EDITION

AVOCATALOG

SUMMER EDITION

AVOCOPTER

AVOCARD DECK

AVOCADOORS

AVOCAR

AVOCARDIGAN

AVOCADOG

AVOCADODO

We can't stop him if we can't get in! We have to get rid of the stinky stuff!

Look . . . a bouncy castle!

FAIRY PINK CAS

That's it! The Fairy Pink Castle—it's perfect!

Yay! I'm so happy you've given up on that whole evil Avocado thing! So, who wants to be my bounce buddy?

FAIRY PINK CASTLE

Given up?! No way!

Who wants to be my suck-all-the-stinky-gas-from-the-gift-shop buddy?!

66

When I unleash my secret weapon at the Avo Great Spray launch party tonight, Walter will hand over the key to the whole waterpark. Then anyone in my way will get . . . popped!

MWAHAHA HAHAHA

AVO GREAT GIFT SHO

Oooh, where did he get that shirt from?

Chapter Eight

Total A-pop-alypse

So how do we stop Avocadon't?

We need to find out what his secret weapon is and block it!

TRAIL OF GREEN GOO

So, who's ready to follow that fruit?!

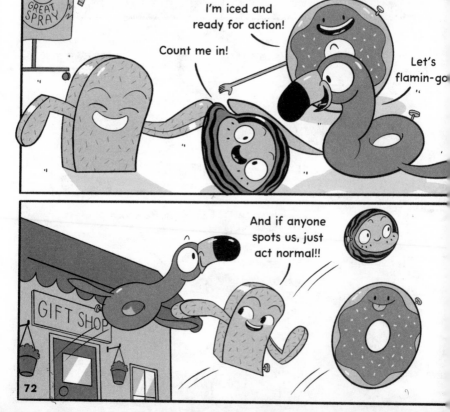

I'm iced and ready for action!

Count me in!

Let's flamin-go!

And if anyone spots us, just act normal!!

GIFT SHOP

75

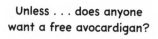

Unless . . . does anyone want a free avocardigan?

Silly me! I forgot to hide the Big Free Avocardigan button.

BIG FREE AVOCARDIGAN BUTTON

It's right by you, Donut. One press and you'll get free avocardigans for life.

And did I mention hot dogs, too?

NOOOOOOOO!

AHHHHHHH!

SLAM!

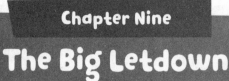

Chapter Nine
The Big Letdown

The Avo Great Launch Party has started! Come and celebrate at the Big Splash Pool!

AVO GREAT SPRAY

LAUNCH PARTY

YUMMY ~~HYPNOTIC~~ GUACAMOLE

AVO GRE
LAUNC

BIG SPLASH POOL

It's over. Avocadon't has outsmarted me.

I'm sorry, inflata-friends.

Goodbye, Have a Great Spray.

Goodbye, happy times.

Goodbye, Lost and Found pool.

And can I just say ho sorry I am about the whole button mix-up

We won't even get to say goodbye to Lynn.

Bow down to the super-stack, you pesky pimento! I take NO prisoners!

And the party looks . . . fun. This is air-rendous.

Don't be sad, Cactus.

You did everything you could!

Avocadon't is just the evilest fruit and/or vegetable EVER!

He doesn't even like hugs.

Or not popping his only friends in the world.

C'mon, Cactus. There's nothing a Donut hug can't fix. Well, maybe it can't make an Avocado go soft, but . . .

You're right. Avocadon't may have an impressively evil brain—

And a great cap collection!

Chapter Ten
It's Nacho Park Anymore

Welcome to MY party. I hope you have a mesmerizing time!

AVO GREAT SPRAY
LAUNCH PARTY

IT'S AVOCADO JEAN. LIVING THE AVOCADO DREAM. WITH MY DE-PITTING MACHINE. AVO GREAT SPRAY!

S. LIDE

Somebody get me a VIP inflatable! And make sure it's got eight cup holders for all my delicious guacamole.

It's time to . . .

Avo Great PARTY!

CAN YOU FIND . . .

☐ Walter's spare flip-flop

☐ Gift Shop Shelly's skateboard

☐ Queen Swanicorn's newly added eighth cup holder

☐ Paws and Claws

☐ Gnaws and Jaws

☐ Ice Cream Jean

☐ Avocado Toast

☐ 'Cado Coaster

95

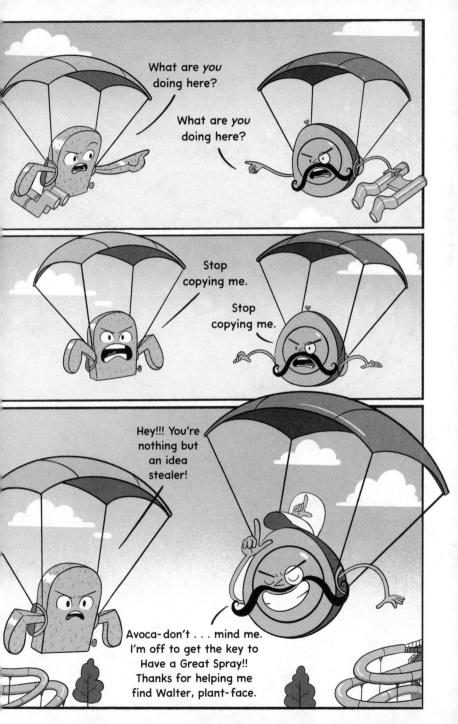

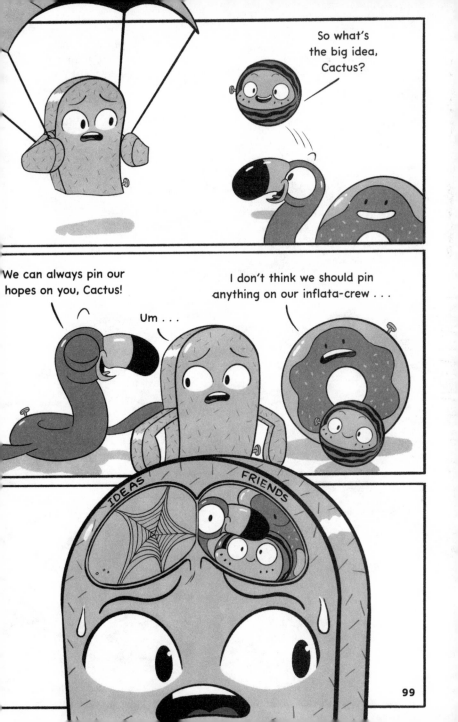

SWOOSH

What about making the world's biggest whirlpool? I could whip one up with my super-speedy skills?

I would help but I was trying Balloon Shape Number 53 - Avocado Masher and now I'm stuck like a statue.

Watermelon, pour in the powder!

Do you need help lifting it?

Do you need help tasting it?

JELL-O POWDER EXTRA STRONG

SETS QUICK!

It's clumping!

We need to mix it up. FAST!

JELL-O POWDER EXTRA STRONG

Time to whip up a storm!

And if anyone knows how to make Jell-O, it's me!

Um . . . it isn't working!

STIR
STIR

Oh no! Walter is handing over the key! We need to make one MEGA wave to stop him!

My game's glitched. And you're the only inflata-genius that can fix it.

We're kind of in the middle of saving the waterpark here!

Yeah. Avocado is really evil . . . and he's hypnotized Walter . . . and he's about to hand over the key to Have a Great Spray . . . and we turned the pool into Jell-O . . . but now we gotta get the key first . . . and it's too sticky to walk on!

STATS

So what I'm hearing is that you need me to build you a path to Walter?

Yes, but we've only got seven seconds before the Jell-O melts!

Nachos stacked in 1.67 seconds.

SHOOP
SHOOP
SHOOP

A personal best.

×4

BOING!   BOING!

Yesssssssssss!

Chapter Twelve

Happily Avo After

And the inflata-gang lived happily avo after.

Wait, no. That's just the guacamole talking.

LOST & FOUND

CRUSH THAT NACHO

zzz

OUT OF MY WAY, KITTEN!

zzz

EVERYTHING BUT CHURROS

FLAMINGO WEEKLY

I can't believe that Jell-O took you a whole week to slurp up, Donut.

I can't believe
I still wasn't ful

115

Maybe she just needs more time to get Nacho Crunch Kitten Crush Saga out of her system.

Did someone say Nacho Crunch Kitten Crush Saga?!

No, absolutely not. I said . . . macho lunch mitten mush car grr.

Um . . . anyway. Lynn, have you ever tried balloon modeling?

BALLOON MODELING FOR DUM DUMS

Does anyone get crunched to a pulp?

No.

Well, then it's not the hobby for me.

Whatever happened to that annoying little avocado, anyway? Sure, he had great gifts, but I didn't like his attitude. Or his mustache.

119

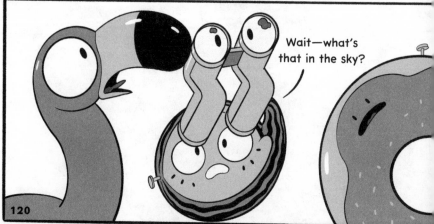

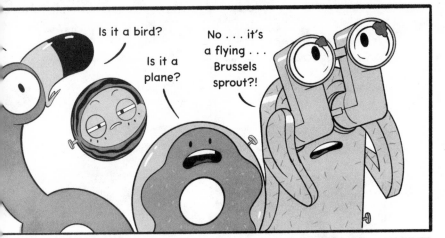

COMING SOON: *DO-NUT PANIC!*

I know something
you don't know.

You know A LOT
we don't know.

Is it something . . . sweet?

I bet it's something fancy.

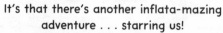

It's that there's another inflata-mazing
adventure . . . starring us!

May I place an order for twel
ice cream sundaes please?

Holey sprinkles! Donut's going on a treasure hunt. The prize? The most delicious cookie ever tasted. But to find it, he needs to sneak his inflata-pals out of the water park, survive shark-infested seas, and take on a petrifying Pickle. Will the holey hero make it back unpopped, or will the cookie crumble once and for all?

HOME BASE

YOUR FAVORITE BOOKS COME TO LIFE IN A BRAND-NEW DIGITAL WORLD!

- Meet your favorite characters
- Play games
- Create your own avatar
- Chat and connect with other fans

- Make your own comics
- Discover new worlds and stories
- And more!

Start your adventure today! Download the **HOME BASE** app and scan this image to unlock exclusive rewards!

SCHOLASTIC.COM/HOMEBASE